UNQUIET WATERS

Unquiet Waters

by

Thana Niveau

Black Shuck Books
www.BlackShuckBooks.co.uk

First published in the UK by Black Shuck Books, 2017

978-1-913038-08-3

Evan had never liked the causeway. He didn't like the water and he certainly didn't like driving this close to it. It was only two miles from the mainland to Galveston Island, but it felt much longer. As a child the drive had seemed endless to him. But then, all journeys had seemed endless when he was trapped in the back seat with his twin sister Lea.

He always tried to see it through her eyes – the causeway, the water, even the island itself. And he always failed. The bay was a dull greenish grey, matching the colour of the polluted Houston sky. But somehow Lea saw beauty in it. The sea and its creatures had fascinated her since their very first trip to the beach.

Evan still remembered it vividly, every detail. The huge ships gliding by out in the Gulf of

Mexico, the seagulls wheeling overhead, occasionally diving down to snatch food from family picnics or steal fishermen's bait. There was the staccato *whirrrr* of fishing lines being cast and the sloshing of waves where the water met the land. And there were the smells. Fish, sea air, barbecue and coconut suntan lotion.

Evan had been sitting on a pile of soft sand, using a plastic spade and bucket to build a castle. In his mind he could see exactly how he wanted it to look, but reality fell some considerable way short of fantasy. The disappointment was crushing. When his clumsy fingers refused to sculpt the delicately crenellated parapet exactly how it should be, he stood up and kicked the whole mess over, deciding it was more fun to be a giant destroying it instead.

The army men he'd placed inside (he'd decided they were time travellers) were helpless against the onslaught of his stomping feet. The largest tower collapsed, burying them in an avalanche of sand. One soldier managed to escape, crawling bravely towards the moat before the rest of the castle met a similar fate. It was fun playing the villain, but after a while Evan began to feel bad for his victims. He hurriedly rescued them from the sand and sent them back to their time machine so they could go home.

Behind him Lea was laughing brightly and when he turned he saw her running towards the lapping waves. They pawed restlessly at the shore, foaming and frothing like boiled, sour milk. Lea tripped and went sprawling in the wet sand, staring around her in amazement. After a while she sat up. Then she reached down and plucked something from the sand. She held it up with a kind of hushed reverence, as though she'd found a sacred artefact.

Evan didn't want to go close to the water, but he was too curious about what she'd found. What if it was part of some pirate's treasure? A gold doubloon or pieces of eight?

But something seemed bent on thwarting all his wishes that day. It was only a seashell.

Lea looked up as he drew near, her eyes wide with excitement. "Look, Evan," she whispered. "It's alive!"

He peered closer and saw that she was right. A mass of wriggling legs emerged from the mouth of the shell. But there wasn't anything special about that.

"It's just a hermit crab," he said with a shrug, all wisdom and experience at the grand age of seven. Seven and nine minutes, he always told grownups. Those nine minutes were important.

The shell was almost as large as Lea's hand and the reddish legs of the creature stretched out, waving in the air inches from her nose. Evan watched, curiously unnerved by the sight. A sudden strange image came to him of her popping the crab into her mouth, shell and all. In his mind he could even hear the sound it would make as she crunched it up, could practically *taste* it. He shuddered, banishing the unwelcome thought.

"It was something else once," Lea said in a strange voice.

"Huh?"

"Somebody threw it away, threw it in the sea. And it became this."

Now she was really creeping him out. She was holding the crab so close to her eyes she was in danger of being blinded by the squirming legs. There was a keenness to her scrutiny that disturbed him, something in her gaze that seemed old and knowing. She was suddenly like another person.

After a while she set the crab down and watched as it scuttled away, vanishing into the white foam of the waves. Lea looked up at Evan, her expression serious. He had the unpleasant sense that some kind of exchange had taken place, some silent communication.

Then the water surged, splashing and soaking her, and she erupted into delighted squeals and giggles as she flung herself into the surf. His sister was back, and whatever had replaced her for a moment was gone.

Evan had never forgotten that strange encounter, and the memory returned with every trip he made to Galveston to see her. They'd both been weird kids, and weird kids grew up to be weird adults. But lately her emails and texts had reached a new level of what could only charitably be called eccentric.

Lea was a field ecologist, buried deep in research on global warming. She'd developed a sudden interest in fossils, asking Evan to go to the Natural Science Museum and photograph all the Cambrian arthropods he could find there. Such arbitrary requests were nothing new, and he didn't really think anything of it. He'd dutifully done as she asked, and found himself enjoying the little excursion as he imagined her there with him. It felt like the old days, when she still lived in Houston and they got to see each other more often.

He'd emailed her the pictures, but never heard back. That wasn't unusual either. She was easily distracted and she often got lost in work, especially when intriguing tangents presented themselves.

However, when he'd texted her a few days later to ask if she was happy with his photos, the response was baffling.

> Thought Anomalocaris or Marrella but not. Archaean Era?? Before?? Maybe from protoplanets. Must show - come see!

He recognised the first name. It was one of the fossils he'd seen at the museum. Other than that, the message might as well have been in Klingon. They never bothered with full sentences when texting, but this was even more pared down than usual. He'd called her back, but wasn't able to get a straight answer about what she wanted to show him. Just that it was incredible and he had to come.

He was at the highest point of the span now, the stretch of road furthest from the water. Ironically, it was the part that made him the most nervous. He could never banish from his mind the intrusive image of the bridge collapsing, of his car plummeting into the churning grey water, gravity pulling him down, down, down.

"It's only about ten feet deep there," Lea had once reassured him. "You could easily swim to the surface and get to the shore."

Easy for her to say. She was more at home in the water than on land. For Evan the very idea of his head being submerged was enough to trigger a sense of panic.

But he knew exactly what to do if his car ever did go in the water. He'd rehearsed it in his mind countless times to drill it in. First he'd unlatch the seatbelt, then try the electric window. If it worked, he'd lower it an inch and let the water slowly trickle in. If the electric window didn't work, he'd climb over the seat and use one of the old-fashioned cranks on the back windows. As the water filled the car, he would stay calm and focus his mind, and as soon as the level reached his chin, he'd take a deep breath, crank the window down the rest of the way and swim out. He could hold his nose and kick his way ten feet to the surface, he was sure of that. Once there he could float or dog-paddle to the pillars of the causeway and wait to be rescued.

Lea had laughed at his escape plan, but only until she realised he was serious. Then her expression had changed to one of pity.

"I could teach you to swim," she'd told him more than once. "Then you wouldn't be so afraid of the water."

"I'm not afraid of the water. I'm afraid of what's *in* the water."

"But there's nothing to be afraid of."

"Oh right, let me guess – the sharks are more afraid of me than I am of them?"

"You're statistically more likely to be struck by lightning than attacked by a shark."

"Fat lot of good those statistics will do me if I'm the unlucky bastard who gets the shark instead of the lightning."

It was a conversation they'd had so many times they could have recited each other's dialogue. He had never even told her the full truth – that it wasn't sharks he was really afraid of. What he saw waiting for him in the water was something else entirely, something with long, clutching arms that would pull him under. Something that would *claim* him.

Galveston was no pristine Caribbean resort with crystal-clear lagoons where you could see everything swimming around your feet. In the dark, briny water of the Gulf of Mexico, there was no way of knowing what had just brushed against your leg, or what you might step on down there.

Lea loved to dive beneath the surface and those momentary disappearances when they were little had caused Evan intense distress. Quite apart from the irrational fear that she would never surface again, he lived in dread of her grabbing his ankles and dragging him down. She'd done it once in a motel swimming pool and that was bad enough. But the idea of vanishing beneath those umber waves himself filled him with horror.

At the top of the span he looked to his left to see the railway line that ran parallel with the modern road. It was the original causeway, over a century old and apparently still used by trains, although Evan had never seen one there. In fact, he'd never even seen the drawbridge lowered. As kids he and Lea had always hoped to race a train to the island, but it was not to be.

The raised drawbridge was another thing Evan didn't like, although he couldn't have said why. Perhaps it was the way the two halves resembled a gaping mouth, like an alligator made of concrete and steel. The new causeway had no drawbridge; the arch was high enough for boats to pass underneath. But that didn't stop him imagining the road suddenly lifting up in front of him, all the traffic smashing headlong into the unyielding wall. It was only once he had finally crested the hill that he could relax.

One night he dreamed he saw a train. The two causeways were much closer together and the new one was only wide enough for his car. The guardrails were missing. He heard the whistle of the approaching locomotive and looked up to see it racing along the tracks. Coming straight towards him. It was going too fast and he was going too slow. There was nowhere for him to go as the train jumped the tracks, its line of cars buckling as it twisted in the air. It came down on the narrow causeway and smashed through, plunging into the water like a sea serpent. Evan tried to brake, but the road followed the train's trajectory, slanting down towards the waves. He woke up just before he fell in.

It had all felt so real, so horribly inevitable, and he couldn't help reliving the nightmare every time he passed the drawbridge. Once he reached the island, his heart rate would go back to normal. He could see whatever it was Lea wanted to show him and they could have a nice lunch. Before that, though, he had to pass one final landmark: the sunken boat.

It had been there for as long as he and Lea could remember. The little fishing boat lay off to the right, among the reeds in the shallows at the edge of the shore. Only a bit of the hull remained now, and the masts jutted from the water like bones. In time there would be nothing left of it at all, and Evan felt an inexplicable pang of sadness at the thought. It was probably an eyesore for most, detritus that had never been cleared away. But, as eerie as it was, it was a fixture of the island for him and Lea.

At last he could see palm trees and the bay gave way to wetlands as he neared the end of the causeway. A heron was stalking through the saltgrass of the marsh. He was safe on dry land once more and he made his way along the main road, catching glimpses of the Gulf down the streets to his right. As he passed the iconic mansion known as Bishop's Palace it suddenly struck him that, in all the years their family had been visiting Galveston, they had never taken the tour inside.

He reached Lea's street and parked outside the little beach house she called home. She'd paid far too much for it, using most of the money from their inheritance. Then she'd squandered even more painting it a vibrant emerald green, only for the colour to fade within a couple of years. Sand, salt and sun were no friend to little wooden boxes. Now the house looked sickly, as did so many others around it. They were like film sets, places built to look like houses, but never actually meant to be lived in.

Still, he had to concede that it had a sort of charm. A slender palm tree grew in front, its trunk curved in a graceful arc. And the vibrant pink bougainvillea that swamped the porch was in full bloom, almost obscuring the little sign that said MERMAID CROSSING. Evan had bought it for her as a joke in one of the tourist shops along the Strand, never imagining she'd hang it up. But he liked that she had.

He'd driven all the way with the car's AC cranked up high, wishing it was actually possible to make himself cold enough that the stifling heat might be tolerable. He shut off the engine and braced himself, then stepped out into the steambath of the island. It was only May and it was already over 100 degrees.

Before he had even closed the car door, Lea was pelting down the wooden stairs and running towards him, arms outstretched. He couldn't help but smile at her exuberance as she flung herself at him in a fierce embrace, the impact causing him to swing her around. One of her flip-flops came off and landed on the hood of his car and they both laughed.

"Wow, it hasn't been that long, has it?"

"It's been ages!" she lamented.

"Yeah, well, you *could* come see *me*, you know."

She didn't reply.

"Never mind," he said softly.

He always suggested it. She never responded. And he never pushed it.

As claustrophobic as the island and the water and the causeway made him feel, the mainland made her feel even worse. She didn't own a car and the one time she had braved the journey to his place in a taxi – at his invitation and expense – she'd been like a small terrified animal that had spent its whole life in a cage and didn't know how to cope in the outside world. It had been awful to see. He'd driven her back himself the same night.

But she was happy here. She was living in the world that had always fascinated her, and the Gulf of Mexico was her backyard. There were shops and restaurants along the seafront, including Casa Mare, a shabby-chic little cafe where they usually ate when he visited. It was only a ten-minute walk away, but as far as Evan was concerned, in the stifling heat of a Texas summer, it might as well be ten miles. But he was willing to endure it for her.

He smiled at Lea and she mirrored his expression. She looked like a vintage movie star in her enormous shades and sun hat. And the white bikini top and cutoffs made her tanned skin appear even darker. Everything about her radiated health and happiness. Physically anyway.

"You've gone totally native," Evan said. Next to her he looked pale and anaemic. No one would ever guess they were twins.

He armed sweat off his forehead as he closed the car door. The sun blazed overhead and he could feel the heat of the driveway through his sandals. Summers here were notoriously brutal, sweltering and sticky with humidity. Even so, houses like Lea's often didn't have air conditioning. He never understood how she could stand it.

She smiled as she retrieved her flip-flop. She didn't bother to put it back on and he winced at the sight of her bare foot on the scorching pavement. He remembered how the blacktop in the school playground used to turn soft in the heat, and the swings and monkey bars were too hot to touch.

Lea took his arm and pulled him towards the house. "Come on," she said. "I can't wait to show you!"

At the top of the stairs she kicked off her remaining flip-flop and dropped the other one beside it on the porch, leaving Evan behind to remove his sandals. Sand gritted under his bare feet as he stepped inside and he made a face. The floor was always sandy. He didn't know why she even bothered with the Buddhist no-shoes thing at all.

He tried to pull the front door closed only for it to bang against the frame and bounce open again. It was hanging crookedly askew, wrenched off its top hinge.

"Lea, your door is…"

But she had vanished into the back.

He peered at the busted hinge for a moment longer before edging back inside, where it was cooler. The ceiling fan was on, listlessly stirring the heavy air. He pulled the chain to make it turn faster.

He didn't need to be told to help himself to coffee. Lea always managed to time it perfectly with his arrival. The aroma was heavenly, but it did little to mask the stronger smell of the sea that permeated the house through the open windows. There was a brisk breeze, but the air itself was like liquid salt. Lea said she found the scent of fish comforting, but to Evan it just smelled like the dumpsters outside a seafood restaurant.

He downed the coffee, sighing with pleasure at the invigorating taste. It was only in the past year that she'd finally gotten it right. Lea never drank coffee herself, so brewing the perfect pot for her brother had always been something of an experiment. He peeked in the cabinet to see what he was drinking and was surprised to find an expensive designer brand he never would have splurged on for himself. But he wasn't going to complain or tell her she shouldn't have. After years of suffering through her lesser efforts, this tiny luxury was only fair.

It took him a moment to register what was odd about the cabinet. Then it clicked. There was nothing to eat. Just a half-empty bag of rice and a couple of cans of tuna, nothing that looked like proper food. His curiosity got the best of him and he decided to look in the refrigerator, only to recoil at the stench. He slammed the door. Whatever was in there was well past its sell-by date. He had a sudden image of rotting bait and buckets of chum sitting out in the heat.

Well, maybe she just ate out all the time. Or she hadn't gone to the store yet for provisions. Maybe it was too hot even for her. He decided not to say anything. Not about the fridge anyway – he was definitely going to ask about the front door.

He was pouring another cup of coffee when she reappeared, bearing a long shallow plastic box, the kind you stored things in under the bed.

She set it on the kitchen table and waved him over. "They're sleeping," she said in a theatrical whisper.

"You know your door is broken?"

She either didn't hear him or didn't care.

"Lea," he said. "Hello? What happened to your door? How long has it been like that?"

She looked up, distracted and annoyed that he was focused on something else. "How long has what – oh, the door. I don't know. Couple of months. The last tropical storm."

"Are you serious? Lea, do you have any idea how dangerous that is? Anyone could come in here! Or any*thing*! Look, all my tools are in the car. Let me just get them and I'll—"

"Leave it!"

He froze, silenced by the ferocity in her voice. He stood staring at her, too stunned to speak.

After a while she forced a little laugh. "Sorry. I just... I really want you to see this. Please?"

Her girlish plea made him relent. And her insistence had actually piqued his curiosity. With a final glance at the door, he crossed to the table and peered into the container. She might have just taken it from the oven, there was so much heat coming off it. Presumably she kept it on the back porch and had only brought it in to spare him the horror of the inhospitable temperature outside. But she'd only saved him from the heat, not the smell. If anything, it was worse than what was in the fridge. He wrinkled his nose and resisted the urge to pinch it shut.

The water was murky, but he could make out the shapes of several tiny pale creatures floating within, each about the size of a grain of rice. They didn't appear to be moving, not of their own volition. The water was still sloshing gently from the movement of the box and the creatures were rocked with the current.

Evan didn't know what to say. He wasn't even sure what he was supposed to be looking at. Frankly, he was far more concerned about the door.

"Now watch," Lea said. She dipped her fingers into a little plastic container and sprinkled some brown flakes into the warm, cloudy water. Nothing happened.

Evan opened his mouth to tell her the things looked dead to him, but she shushed him before he could speak. He sighed and turned his attention back to the water.

After a few moments he thought he saw one

of them twitch, just a whisper of movement. Lea's little gasp told him this was the reaction she'd been expecting. Another creature jerked and darted across the water, leaving a tiny V-shaped wake behind it. One by one the others began to stir, scurrying around in the water. He could make out the flicker of tiny legs.

Lea looked overjoyed, but her excitement was way out of proportion to what had just occurred.

"So..." he ventured, "you gave fish food to some bugs and they woke up and swam around?"

Her expression hardened and she stared at Evan as though he were a stranger. "They're not bugs," she snapped.

For a moment it seemed like she wasn't going to explain further and he felt like the rug had been pulled out from under him. He'd clearly offended her, but he was totally in the dark. "Look, I'm sorry, but I have no idea what I'm supposed to be seeing here. You're the expert. You tell me what's so amazing about it."

"They're alive," she said, her eyes shining.

"I can see that. And?"

"They shouldn't be."

Evan was beginning to wonder whether this was some kind of practical joke. He'd driven all the way out here for *this?* He raised his eyebrows enquiringly, waiting for her to elaborate.

"Do you know what was in that water before?" She gazed down at the box.

"Judging from the smell, quite a lot of dead fish?"

Lea shook her head. "Nothing alive or dead. Nothing organic at all. It's just water from the Gulf." She peered closely into his eyes, as though anticipating a breakthrough on his part. "Polluted water from the Gulf," she added.

Evan was tiring of the game. He pulled his T-shirt away from where it had stuck to his chest and stood beneath the fan. "You're going to have to spell it out for me," he said wearily.

She dropped into a chair with a sigh. "Sorry. I forget sometimes you're not actually here with me."

He frowned at the odd admission, but he knew what she meant. He talked to her also when he was on his own. Only in his case there was no answering voice. He suspected Lea had a version of him with her all the time, who listened to her manic chatter and understood it. His eyes flicked again to the broken door.

"Just start at the beginning," he urged, tilting his head back to feel the breeze on his face.

"Yes. Okay. The beginning." She seemed to notice his discomfort for the first time. She got up and went to the fridge, and he braced himself for the smell. But instead she opened the door to the freezer, filled a glass with ice cubes and handed it to him.

He rubbed the glass gratefully across his forehead and over the back of his neck. No wonder she was so scattered; the heat was probably cooking her brain. He noticed that the sky had darkened with clouds. Rain would only increase the appalling humidity, but at least it might cool things down a little.

"Do you remember the first time we went to the beach?" Lea asked.

"I've never forgotten it."

"Do you remember that little Vietnamese girl?"

He nodded. He'd never forgotten her either.

After the weirdness with Lea and the crab, Evan had gone back to the sand, determined to build a new castle. Suddenly a scream rang out, as piercing as a siren. Sleeping sunbathers bolted upright, staring around, looking for the source of the cries.

The little girl had been splashing in the

shallow water not far from Lea and she had stepped on a piece of glass. Except it was more than just a piece of glass. It was half a broken liquor bottle, the kind a thug might use to carve up someone's face in a bar fight. The glass had gone straight through her foot like a huge, vicious fang and the girl was screaming at the top of her lungs as she lay where she'd fallen.

It was as though someone had yelled "Shark!" Her screams brought everyone out of the water at full pelt, even Lea. When the grownups realised what had happened, they clustered around the girl and her parents, who were shouting for someone in the gawking crowd to call an ambulance.

There wasn't much the lifeguard could do and the bottle was wedged so far into the girl's foot he advised them to leave it for the ambulance crew to remove. Or the surgeon in the hospital she was destined for.

Evan shuddered. "Yeah, I remember her."

"Well, the same thing happened to me a couple of weeks ago."

At his look of horror she was quick to add, "Oh, not as bad as her, don't worry. I got back here and managed to get all the glass out of my foot. At least I thought I did. I'm writing about the impact of climate change on the barrier islands so I've been doing some tests on the water. Do you know how polluted the Gulf of Mexico is?"

Evan held up his hands. "Focus, Lea."

"Yeah, sorry. Okay, so a couple of days later, my foot got infected and I realised there were still some pieces of glass in it. I thought soaking it in seawater might help, so I did that."

Evan had forgotten all about his own discomfort. "What? Why didn't you go to a doctor?"

She shrugged. "No insurance. Besides, I didn't think it was that big a deal. Anyway, I fell asleep with my foot in one of those containers and when I woke up I was fine. The water was all bloody and there were little shards of glass at the bottom, and my foot was healed." Lea returned to the table and looked down at the things swimming in the box. "The next day, they appeared."

Evan followed her gaze and watched the creatures. They were livelier now and there was something oddly focused about their movements. It bothered him.

"They should have pulled that bottle out of the girl's foot," Lea mused, sounding far away. "They should have given it back."

He didn't like the glazed look in her eyes, the awe in her voice. She sounded like someone who'd joined a cult.

"What are you telling me?" he asked cautiously.

She lifted her head, a smile playing across her features. "I took something from the ocean. So the ocean took something from me. And together we made something new."

It had to be the heat making her crazy. That or the infection had been worse than she thought. He heard the echo of her voice all those years ago.

It was something else once. Somebody threw it away, threw it in the sea. And it became this.

Evan turned away. He set the glass of melting ice cubes on the counter and looked out the window. The leaves were wet and he realised it had been raining for some time. The rain drummed on the roof like impatient fingers, but it couldn't drown out the seagulls or the churning surf. The smell of rotting fish was starting to make his head spin. From here the water looked like chocolate milk and he felt nauseated at the thought of his sister immersing herself in it day after day. How could they be so different? How could they look at that stretch of beach and see such entirely different worlds?

He rubbed his temples as he tried to think of what to say. Dredging his memory unearthed another unpleasant nugget of weirdness and the pieces began to fall into place.

When they were kids, the beach and dunes had always been littered with trash, especially cans, bottles and those plastic yokes that held six-packs together. There was one day in particular when it seemed as if a garbage truck had overturned. They'd been about ten, Evan guessed, walking along the shore looking for seashells when they saw what looked like a plastic bag half-buried in the sand. It billowed a little in the breeze.

But as they drew nearer they realised it was a jellyfish. Lea immediately grabbed a long piece of driftwood and speared the creature's body, hoisting it high in the air.

Evan dodged away from her. "What are you doing?"

"I'm putting it back where it belongs," Lea stated matter-of-factly. "In the sea."

Evan shuddered. A dead jellyfish was just as dangerous as a living one, still capable of burning you with its stinging tentacles.

"I think you should leave it where people can see it."

But Lea wouldn't be deterred. She held the stick high overhead and the jellyfish dangled above her like a flag. She looked like a knight carrying a banner into battle as she marched towards the water's edge.

Evan held his breath, waiting for the creature to fall, to drop onto her head. Or slide down the stick onto her hands.

Perhaps it wasn't dead. He didn't like the way the gelatinous body resembled a huge, glazed eye. Was it watching him now?

"The sea gets lonely," Lea said. "If I put it back, she might turn it into something else."

These were ideas she had been obsessing over her whole life. How could Evan not have seen it? All at once he felt the crushing weight of guilt. He knew her better than anyone. He should have come out here more often, pushed aside his own neurotic fear about the stupid causeway. Instead he'd let her isolate herself on this island, in this squalid little shack, where her hold on reality had only gotten more slippery as the years went by.

He pictured her holed up in here while a hurricane lashed the trees outside and threw thirty-foot waves against the seawall. The island was already sinking as the sea levels rose. How long would it be before the foul waters swallowed the whole house? She said the door had been busted since the last tropical storm. He shuddered to think who or what might have been able to just waltz right in while she slept. If she slept at all. Maybe she just sat up all night staring into buckets full of toxic waste, waiting for creatures to pop out and say hi. Maybe the open door was an invitation for something to come in from the sea.

There was a click as the ice cubes shifted in his glass, and he felt as though someone had dropped one down the back of his shirt. He didn't think those flakes she had dropped into the water were fish food. The heat, the smell, the sickening realisation... All at once he felt dizzy. His stomach lurched and his voice was little more than a hoarse croak as he told her he needed the bathroom.

He rushed from the kitchen and got there

just in time to fall to his knees before the toilet. He hadn't eaten anything that morning and last night's beer tasted horrible on the way back up. After a few wretched heaves, he flushed the toilet and confronted his haggard reflection in the mirror. He ran the faucet and splashed cold water in his face and over his head, wishing the refreshing sensation would never end.

"You okay in there?" Lea called.

"I'm fine! Just... the heat, you know? I'll be out in a few minutes."

He listened as she padded away. Then he opened the door and slipped quietly down the hall, into her bedroom. There was something he needed to see. The rain was coming down harder and a gust of wind rustled some loose papers somewhere in the room. It sounded like claws.

Her laptop sat on a little table against the wall. It was open and a screensaver was dancing over the cracked screen. Evan tapped the trackpad and a document appeared. He assumed the confusing text that greeted him was a table with equations or chemical formulae. He scrolled to the beginning and began to read.

The Poisoned Wellspring: The Real Impact of Climate Change on the Ocean

4.56 billion years ago an immense cloud began to coalesce, spin and collapse under its own gravity in a process known as cold accretion. This solar nebula was the origin of our solar system. The orbiting chunks of rock and ice eventually became the four inner planets, and in what was still the infancy of the Earth, oceans began to form. Saltwater seas have dominated our planet for 3.5 billion years and they are the source of all life here. All *indigenous* life.

But just as intergalactic elements influenced the birth and development of our sun and planets, so too has Earth's dominant species played a part in the development of other forms of life.

Between 50 and 80% of all life on Earth exists in the ocean, but alongside the 1.5 million species that are known, there are potentially 50 million as yet undiscovered.

More statistics followed, with detailed information on mankind's impact on the planet's ecosystems, the melting of the ice caps and the rising sea levels. She speculated about the existence of distant planets with no land masses at all, where aquatic life could flourish.

He began to skim, but he was brought up short by the word "sea-monkeys". After a moment's confusion, he saw she was describing the process by which the little brine shrimp were awakened from their dormant, desiccated state by adding "instant life eggs" to their environment. He couldn't help but smile at the memory of the sea-monkey tank they had kept when they were little. It was probably many kids' introduction to the concept of false advertising.

But his smile vanished as Lea began describing her own similar process of reviving life forms from a cryptobiotic state.

> The combination of global warming and pollution has created a reaction chamber for these organisms, most of which have been inactive for billions of years. Now many more are beginning to awaken.

As he read on, it became clear that she wasn't talking about the fossilised remains of prehistoric species; she was talking about life that had come from elsewhere in the universe, organisms trapped inside the rocks and space dust that had formed the solar system. They had survived the journey and the incomprehensibly long sleep and now mankind's contamination of the planet was actually aiding in their rebirth.

One phrase bothered him especially: "most of which have been inactive." Was she seriously suggesting that aliens had been living among us for aeons?

"Oh, Lea," he said softly.

As it went on, the paper began to lose its objectivity, and its way. He caught the word "mermaid" at one point, but couldn't find the context for it. Several times she referred to the ocean as though it was alive itself and consciously nurturing both the creatures and the toxins inside it. There was her familiar theme about replacing what had been taken from the water so that it could transform. She talked as though the ocean itself wanted to transform, to drown the world. To reclaim it.

He saw a list of dates and numbers, with vague descriptions of the things he had seen flitting in the container. Something about the process of stimulating them had seemed oddly familiar to him at the time, but he hadn't made the connection with sea-monkeys. He knew almost nothing about the science behind this stuff, but if there were some 50 million unknown species in the ocean, then surely it made more sense that Lea had discovered one of those rather than something that travelled here from the far distant stars. Something that could be awakened just like those little brine shrimp.

Other odd phrases caught his eye as he continued to scroll through.

> Eutrophication of the water triggered the Late Devonian mass extinction, wiping out three-quarters of all life on Earth. Now, as a result of the levels of pollution, a similar over-abundance of nutrients in the water is causing other species to thrive. One creature's poison is another's sustenance. And we are their "instant life eggs". As the sea levels rise, so will they.

It was all beginning to sound sinister and apocalyptic. And his heart twisted as he realised it went on like that, page after page of escalating madness. Evan couldn't take any more. He closed the laptop gently and rested his hand on its warm surface before turning away, only to flinch at the sight of the room before him.

It was a shambles. The open window had allowed both rain and seawater to saturate the wall beneath it. Books and papers lay scattered across every surface, spilling onto the floor. Figurines had been blown off the shelves by the wind and never put away.

The bed was unmade, the sheet thrown back. And what he saw there made his skin crawl. It was full of sand. Not just a few grains either; she must have scooped up buckets of it and dumped it in her bed. Tears pricked his eyes and he turned to go, but a flicker of movement made him stop.

He didn't want to look, but he forced himself to move closer to the bed. There was something moving in the sand. A chill went through him as he realised not just what he was seeing, but what he had been hearing.

These were larger than the ones she had woken for him, and entirely translucent. She had mentioned crabs and sea-spiders in her paper, and they resembled both as they clambered through the wasteland where she slept. Each was about the size of his hand, with a soft, segmented body and rounded flaps down each side that looked more suited to swimming than crawling on land. Two long spines extended backward from the head, and the creatures tracked his movement as he inched closer to the bed. As one, they scuttled towards the edge of the mattress, stretching their antennae towards him.

Outside, the storm sounded like a woman screaming.

He'd seen enough. He rubbed away the prickling sensation on the back of his neck, steeling himself as he returned to the kitchen.

Lea was standing over the container as if she'd never moved, still watching in fascination as the little creatures swam back and forth in patterns that she probably believed were attempts to communicate.

"Come on," he said, taking her gently by the arm. "We have to go."

She blinked in surprise. "What do you mean? You just got here. I thought we were going to have lunch."

He silently blessed her for providing the means to a perfect lie. "Exactly. I haven't eaten anything all day and I'm starved."

She looked puzzled as he took out his car keys. "But Casa Mare is so close. We can walk—"

"It's raining, silly. Can't you hear it?"

She looked up and he saw her register the sound. She smiled, but it was a pale imitation of the one she'd shown earlier, when he'd first arrived. That seemed like years ago.

He slipped his sandals on in the doorway. "It's okay," he said. "I don't mind driving. Besides, I wanted to go to the Strand anyway."

"Oh. Okay."

It was all he could do not to wilt with relief at her trusting compliance. As he led her down the stairs, through the rain and into the car, he felt like the villain in some old movie, luring the wide-eyed heroine to the asylum. Well, she could curse his tactics later, but there was no question that he had to get her away from this place. Away from the house, the water, the island. Most of all away from those... things.

They were both drenched by the time they were settled in the car. Lea had thrown a flimsy shirt over her bikini top but she didn't even seem to notice that she was still barefoot. Evan said nothing. He wasn't even sure where to take her. There was probably a hospital in Galveston, but he didn't know where it was and in any case he wanted her off the island.

The sky had darkened and the car rocked from side to side as the wind threw waves of rain against it. This was more than just a monsoon. There hadn't been any weather warnings on the radio as he was driving over. But then, as always, he had been preoccupied.

He retraced the route he had taken to get to her house, hoping she was too out of it to notice he wasn't going in the direction of the Strand. The windshield wipers were having a hard time keeping up with the deluge and when he glanced down a side street he saw white-capped waves leaping in the Gulf. Surely it was some trick of the light that made them look as high as the houses.

Lea didn't say a word and her silence was even more disturbing than her fervent rambling. He'd expected her to freak out when she realised he was lying about where he was taking her. Instead, she was simply gazing out the passenger window. She was watching the same violent storm he was, but nothing about it seemed to faze her.

Evan was terrified. It was one thing to hold the car steady driving through gale-force winds on a road on the island, quite another to have to make it across the causeway in such conditions.

It's only two miles, he reminded himself. That was true, but reaching the mainland wasn't going to make the storm magically abate. Once there, he'd still have the problem of what to do with his sister.

One thing at a time.

When the causeway finally came into view, he felt light-headed. But he put his foot down and barrelled ahead, refusing to look at anything but the line of road in front of him. He couldn't maintain the speed for long, as the route was clogged with slow-moving traffic. He wanted to scream with frustration as he was forced to slow to a crawl.

The palm trees on either side were whipping back and forth, bent double in the fury of the storm, ready to snap like matchsticks at any second. Then they were past them, past the salt marsh, and out over the open water. The bay rippled around and beneath the causeway like a black carpet.

"The boat."

Lea's voice was so soft he wasn't sure she had even spoken.

"What boat?"

He risked a glance at her and saw she was looking off to his left. As though exploiting his lapse in attention, the car swerved a little, pushed by a powerful gust of wind. He clutched the steering wheel and regained control, holding it steady as they edged further out onto the causeway.

"The sunken boat. It's gone."

Her words chilled him to the core. He desperately wished he could just jam his foot down on the accelerator, push the car up to 100 and rocket past all the other vehicles. Being trapped at this snail's pace with them was maddening. He had to outrun the storm. He also couldn't shake the feeling that it wasn't just the storm that was chasing them.

He was approaching the top of the span, the point he hated the most. Thunderheads loomed over the bay and the water appeared to be boiling. Huge curtains of rain swept across the lines of cars. Lightning carved a jagged path through the black clouds and a deafening crack of thunder followed instantly.

The noise made Lea jump and she suddenly sat up, her eyes wide as she stared around, seeming to realise for the first time where they were. "Evan? What are you doing?"

His fingers contracted, clutching the steering wheel tightly as he tried to will the traffic to move, to drive, to get off the causeway. He tried to make himself smile for her sake. "I'm taking you to my place," he said. "We'll be safe there."

She stared at him for a moment, her expression fearful. "You can't take me away from here. The sea won't let you. It's part of me now."

He shook his head, wishing he could tune out her words. The traffic had come to a standstill at the crest of the hill and the position gave him a view he would rather not have had. Horns blared as people became frantic, but they were trapped, just like Evan was.

Lea continued, her voice calm, her eyes shining with unnatural intensity. "I gave myself to the water. I've been drinking it. And they've been drinking *me*."

Her words made him feel sick. The rain had become hail, battering the windshield like pebbles. It was all he could do to stay calm as dark waves rose below the causeway, surging high enough to send spray up onto the road. Stranded fish flopped on the concrete.

"Go, go, go," he urged the other drivers. "Please move!"

"It won't let you leave," Lea said again.

"Well, I'm damn well going to try!" he shot back.

But there was no way out of the gridlock. Occasionally he was able to creep forward a few inches, but there was clearly some obstacle at the far end. Around him he saw people start to panic, abandoning their cars and running, stranding everyone else behind the roadblock of deserted vehicles. A man and woman pulled their two small children out of the stalled Volkswagen beside him and fled down the causeway.

Another bolt of lightning ripped the sky apart with an explosion that made Evan cover his ears. He watched in helpless horror as the leaping waves gained strength until one massive surge crashed over the causeway and swept the family over the side. His stomach plunged.

Above them the clouds had massed together, fusing into an enormous storm wall, sharply pointed at one end. Evan knew the danger signs. Anyone who'd grown up here would recognise that formation. They had no choice but to run.

"Come on, Lea, we have to get out of here before—"

But it was too late. The tornado dropped out of the cloud like a spike. It slammed straight down onto the railway, wrenching apart the girders of the drawbridge and sending them flying in all directions. The impact was deafening, almost drowning out the shrieking of the wind. It felt like an earthquake, and cracks began scurrying across the causeway. The road buckled, undulating impossibly, the motion sending stalled cars sliding and slamming into one another. Evan tried not to watch as people were trapped between them.

The waves didn't discriminate. They took both people and vehicles, pulling them off the road and into the watery hell below. For a split second he remembered his escape plan and had to bite back a deranged laugh at the thought of calmly winding down the window and swimming free of the maelstrom.

The tornado coiled and twisted, and at first it seemed to be dancing away from the causeway.

Then, as though changing its mind, it paused. And turned.

That was all the motivation Evan needed. He shouldered the door open against the pressure of the wind and grabbed Lea's hands, dragging her out of the car. The strength of the wind was unbelievable; it was like trying to push through a brick wall.

Lea shouted something, but he couldn't hear her over the noise of the storm. He'd always been told that a tornado sounded like a freight train. And it did. It was the train from his nightmare, the one that jumped the track and smashed into the causeway.

Waves leapt and crashed around them as Evan tried to run, yanking at Lea to get her to move. But she refused to go. He grabbed her in desperation and shook her, screaming her name. But she only gazed at him impassively, the picture of calm acceptance. He heard her next words clearly, and he had to wonder if she had even spoken aloud at all.

"If you take something from the ocean, it will take something from you."

His heart sank as he realised she was referring to herself. He made a last attempt to pull her along the road, but she seemed to have the weight of the whole island behind her. He felt her hand slip from his, and before he could grab her again, a column of water rose from the vortex at the base of the tornado. It climbed higher and higher, a boiling wall of liquid darkness, reaching the height of the causeway before arching and falling, raining down on Lea like a giant hand.

Evan screamed as Lea vanished from sight and the force of the splash slammed him into the crash barrier. He scrambled to his feet and ran to the side, clinging to the guardrail as he looked down into the waves. But Lea was gone. There was nothing down there but churning black water.

He was too overwhelmed to notice at first, but the wind had died down. The tornado had thinned to a dancing string and was only stirring up the smallest waves.

Evan stared down into the sea, searching in desperation for any sign of Lea. As the choppy surface smoothed into a flat grey plane, a swirl of terrible colour moved in the darkness below. Something was taking shape. It had a strange, unnatural gleam, like a spill of oil. It grew in size as it rose towards the surface and he thought he saw the flick of a large tail.

Evan stood frozen at the edge of the ruined causeway, trembling. He remembered the word he'd seen in her paper that he couldn't find a context for. Now he thought he understood. If flakes of Lea's dried blood had revived those alien creatures, what might her whole body awaken when fed to the poisoned ocean? What might she become herself?

He continued to watch as the humanoid shape darted beneath the surface, and something in its oily rainbow sheen felt like a message. But what it might be saying, he couldn't begin to guess.

The Reflection

Allan's eyes flew open in the dark, his arms flailing in desperation as he struggled against the water. He clutched frantically, as though he might climb the endless wall of it, somehow scramble up on top of it. But the water only slipped through his fingers, intangible and overwhelming.

It closed over his head, flooding his mouth, his throat, his lungs. A liquid violation. He fought, feeling the icy cold as it began to flow through him, replacing his blood. His skin burned as it began to dissolve, fizzing into bubbles around him. He was sinking.

His eyes fixed on one final sight before his vision began to fade. There was only a moment to register the full horror of what he saw before a scream tore him from sleep.

Wide awake at last, Allan gasped and clutched at his chest, panting and choking. He expected to cough up water, but there was nothing. It had only been a dream. The same dream he'd been having every night for weeks.

When he finally managed to calm down, he replayed the nightmare in his mind. It was always the same. The drowning, the desperation, the terror. But this time he remembered a little more. This time he finally understood. And he felt sick with the realisation of a single terrible truth: someone wanted him dead.

He didn't dare turn on the light. But he didn't dare lie there alone in the blackness either, his eyes so wide it was painful. Someone – or something – might be standing right there, bending over him, inches from his face.

For long minutes he lay in an agony of indecision, breathing hard whilst trying not to, willing his pounding heart to slow. Blood roared in his ears, deafening him.

After what seemed like hours, his body finally tired of the stress of maintaining the sense of panic and began to calm itself. Rationality returned as his fear lessened and the dream imagery began to fade into the background of his mind.

It was just a dream, he told himself. And he was awake now. That was all that mattered.

But even once he was up and about, the single most disturbing aspect of the dream refused to fade. He could still see it as clearly as anything in the world around him.

The man who had his face.

Allan didn't want to go in to work, but he was too unnerved to stay at home. He'd already glimpsed more shadows in the corners than his flat could possibly contain. More than once he'd jumped, convinced he'd heard a whisper behind him. Once even a soft laugh.

There's no one there, he told himself firmly. *No one but your own weird head playing sick games with you.*

He missed the bus, which only further soured his mood. The air was damp and chilly and he zipped up his coat as he stood waiting for the next one. For fifteen minutes he watched as bus after bus trundled along the road, some stopping for passengers, others continuing on. He counted four separate buses all bearing the same route number before his own finally arrived. By then it had started to rain.

There were no familiar faces on board and he felt slightly unnerved by it. As a boy he'd once got on the wrong bus without realising it. He'd kept expecting the unfamiliar streets to resolve into places he knew any moment. Minutes passed in anxious anticipation as the bus carried on, but his surroundings only grew more and more alien. When he finally got up the nerve to ask the driver where they were, he was rewarded with a scornful laugh and a telling-off. He'd been paranoid about the same thing happening ever since.

But the streets he passed this morning were the ones he saw every day. He knew exactly where he was. Even so, something was nagging at his mind, and he sat throughout the journey in an uneasy silence.

When his stop came up he pushed the button and the bus shuddered to a halt. No one else got off with him, which was a bit odd. But then, he reminded himself, this wasn't his usual bus and he wasn't usually this late.

As he did on most mornings, he headed straight for the coffee shop on the corner. The sky had opened and he hadn't brought an umbrella, so he was drenched by the time he arrived and dodged inside out of the downpour. The shop was nearly empty, which made for a nice change. Even nicer – Aneta was behind the counter. For once he'd have the pretty girl all to himself. She didn't notice him at first, as she was bending down to refill the pastry case with blueberry muffins.

He was tempted to ask her for one today. Just to spend an extra few seconds with her. "Good morning," he said, smiling.

Aneta stood up and looked at him, a curious expression on her face. "Allan. Hi. Again."

"Again?"

"Well, you were just here."

"Erm, no."

Aneta glanced around the coffee shop, frowning, and Allan did the same, not really sure what either one of them was looking for. Someone wearing an identical shirt perhaps? Some other guy with glasses and shaggy blond hair?

When her scan proved fruitless, Aneta turned back to Allan. "You were," she insisted.

Allan was completely at a loss. He shook his head, bewildered. "I promise you I wasn't. I've only just got here."

But Aneta was adamant. "Yes. You ordered your usual Death By Caffeine three-shot espresso and you also got a blueberry muffin. Then you left."

Allan felt his skin crawl and a dizzying sense of déjà vu washed over him. He couldn't have ordered a blueberry muffin. He didn't even *like* them; he'd only considered it as an excuse to share another handful of words with her.

"When was this?"

"Ten minutes? Maybe a bit more."

He turned around to look behind him, still baffled by the confusion. She must be mistaken. If he'd been here at his usual time, the shop would have been full of morning commuters, as it was every day. The poor girl was probably just tired and overworked. She'd confused yesterday's encounter with today's.

And the blueberry muffin? The one you only thought *about ordering?*

That was easy to explain. Someone else had ordered one. He felt a little deflated at the thought that he was so unmemorable to her.

"Sorry," he said, looking for something – anything – to say. "I... didn't sleep well."

Aneta smiled as though that cleared

everything up. "No wonder you need more coffee," she said brightly.

But the very thought of it made him feel queasy. "Actually, I think I'll skip it today." Then he corrected himself. "I mean – I've already had enough this morning." He made himself smile as he backed away from the counter.

If the girl looked concerned, she didn't have time to say anything to him about it. A group of rowdy young women had just come in, shaking damp umbrellas in the doorway. The first of them was already at the counter, waiting to be served. As Aneta asked her what she wanted, Allan slipped out of the shop.

The dream. He couldn't remember the details exactly, but tiny glimpses seemed peppered across his mind like drops of water. The deepest and most troubling of them was the image of the man with his face.

Feeling as if he were still dreaming, Allan made his way down the street, his shoulders hunched against the icy needles of rain. It wasn't far to go, but he was soaked anew by the time he reached the nondescript office building. He stood dripping on the floor of the lift, ignoring the scowl from his fellow passenger, a man with an expensive-looking attache case. The two men rode up in silence until the lift stopped at the fourth floor and Allan got off.

Once there, he stood for a while looking through the glass doors leading into the tech support department where he worked. Past his own drowned-rat reflection, he could see the maze of grey cubicles filled with people wearing headsets and talking. Most of them looked bored. A few were milling about, chatting or carrying reports or mugs of coffee.

Allan cupped his hands around his face and peered through the glass. From where he stood, he could just make out the top edge of his own cubicle on the far side of the room, but he couldn't tell if anyone was inside it or not.

A sudden *bang* nearly stopped his heart and he leapt away from the door. But it was only his coworker Simon, knocking on the glass and waving at him from inside the busy office. Allan gave a desultory wave in return and Simon gestured theatrically, as though inviting royalty in.

With great reluctance, Allan pushed the door open and went inside.

"Jesus, man, did you swim here?" Simon asked, laughing.

Allan nodded even though he hadn't actually heard the question. "Yeah." He eyed the far corner of the room, feeling nervous, expectant. Although of what exactly, he wasn't sure.

"You look terrible."

"Huh? Oh, yeah. Guess I'm just feeling a bit under the weather."

"You should have stayed home. I don't want your bloody cold."

"I'm not contagious," Allan grumbled.

Simon looked slightly wounded. "Hey, I was only joking. No need to bite my head off." With that, Simon turned and left, giving Allan no time to apologise.

He stood staring after his friend before his eyes were drawn back to the end of the office where his own cubicle was. For a while he wasn't sure what he was going to do, but then his legs seemed to move of their own accord and before he knew it, he was standing at his desk. His computer was on. Waves of colour pulsed on the monitor, like tentacles trying to escape from their pixelated prison. The screen saver only came on after fifteen minutes of inactivity, which meant the computer had been on for at least that long.

"Morning, Allan!"

The voice made him jump and he looked behind him, but the woman who had called out to him had already gone past. Behind him the window streamed with rain and he could have sworn he felt the floor shift like a ship in a storm.

This is insane, he thought.

With great reluctance he nudged the mouse, waking the computer up. The screen saver vanished and was replaced by a screen showing his personal email account. Open. A chill went through him, like a trickle of icewater through his veins. No one else knew his password. No one could have signed in but him.

He looked around, peering over the top of the cubicle wall. He felt like a hunted animal. Backing away from the desk, he stumbled over his chair and nearly fell. He regained his balance and plunged out into the office, stumbling down the corridor. He didn't know where he was going. There was nowhere he could really hide to spy on his cubicle and wait for the impostor to show himself. But he didn't have to.

Allan Walker was standing right there.

It was a strange and terrifying experience to see himself from the back, as though he'd somehow left his own body. He had to pat himself down to make sure he still had physical form himself. He did. He was real. He existed.

So who – or what – was *that*?

He stood staring for long moments at the man dressed exactly like him, with the exact same hair and build. The double didn't seem to be doing anything, just standing there in the middle of the corridor. Doors were closed on either side and Allan felt a sick sense of dread at the thought of one of them opening suddenly to reveal a person who would think the double was the real Allan Walker.

"Hey!"

Allan thought he had shouted the word but it only came out as a croak. He took a step closer, intent on grabbing the impostor by the shoulder and spinning him round.

"Hey you!"

This time he managed to raise his voice but the figure in the corridor didn't respond. It just stood there, eerily still and silent.

Allan swallowed his unease and took a step closer. The double moved with him, mirroring his action, although he couldn't possibly have seen Allan move behind him. Allan took another step and his double did likewise. For one crazy moment Allan imagined pursuing him like this forever, never able to catch up with the impostor who was always just a few steps ahead.

And what if he did catch up? What if he spun the double around to face him, only to find himself spinning as well, turning to face a different double, who was turning to face yet another behind him, and another behind that one? The thought of made him feel queasy.

He cleared his throat loudly. "Turn around. I want to talk to you."

If the double heard, he gave no sign. There was a fire escape door at the end of the corridor and if he continued to copy Allan's actions they would soon be in the stairwell. Allan didn't like the idea of being in the cold, enclosed space with him, but he was inexplicably terrified of anyone else seeing the double. He had the sense that he would lose himself once someone mistook the impostor for him.

He marched towards the double, who mimicked his purposeful gait and then opened the door to the stairwell. Allan followed him in, wincing as icy water dripped down on him from the ceiling. The landing was slippery and he looked down to see a puddle there. The water distorted his reflection unpleasantly. Once the door swung shut behind him, Allan stopped. The double stopped too, halfway up the first flight of steps.

"Now can we talk?" Allan asked. "At least look at me."

Slowly the double began to turn his head to look down at Allan, a gesture filled with such menace that Allan felt the hairs on the back of his neck begin to bristle. His heart trembled, like that of a cornered rabbit. The double was grinning. And the face that leered at him was his very own. It was like looking in a mirror. Or *through* a mirror. He was almost grateful for the sound of the dripping water, as the silence would have been too awful to bear.

When Allan spoke again his voice was barely a whisper. "What do you want?"

The double didn't reply. He just kept grinning, his mouth stretched wide with clownish malevolence. Then he raised his hand. At first Allan expected to see a weapon, and he was ready to dart back through the door. But the double's hand was empty. Then the fingers curled into the palm, all except for one. The index finger pointed straight at Allan.

Seconds passed like minutes as Allan stood there, staring in horror at the man who looked just like him. He felt dizzy, as though the stairwell had begun to warp around them both. The floor was like wet rubber, soft and insubstantial beneath his feet. Then the double began to move towards him, advancing back down the stairs at an unnervingly unhurried pace.

Allan's heart hammered against his ribs and he reached behind him for the handle of the door. But his clammy fingers couldn't seem to find it. He didn't dare turn away from the double, who was getting closer every moment.

Panic began to creep in. "What do you want?" he shouted, still flailing helplessly at the door. "Who are you? *What* are you?"

But the double only grinned, continuing its relentless descent towards Allan, finger still pointing as if in answer to both questions.

One more step and it would reach the landing. Allan darted a quick look behind him at the door and gave a little cry when he saw that the handle was no longer there. He slammed the heel of his hand into it and gasped as it sank ineffectually into what had once been solid matter. Now it seemed to be melting.

The dripping water increased in tempo, soaking Allan as he edged away. It cascaded down the stairs like a waterfall, and the puddle had risen to his ankles.

The double was right behind him now, so close Allan could feel the heat from its body. It was all wrong, that heat. The thing couldn't possibly be alive. It was just something his mind had conjured. A nightmare, hallucination, anything but what it looked like. And what it looked like was *him*.

"Leave me alone!" he screamed. He tore himself away from the door and flung himself down the stairs, splashing down them as they twisted and writhed beneath his feet.

When he reached the first turning, he looked up to see the double still advancing. Still grinning. Still pointing.

Allan clung to the banister as he pulled himself down through the rushing water. The double seemed unaffected by the distortion of the stairwell. It moved all around Allan like liquid but remained solid for the double. The sudden terrible thought came to him that perhaps he himself was the anomaly, the reflection. What if the man pursuing him was actually Allan Walker? Who was *he*, then?

He reached the next landing and his heart sank when he saw that this one had no door at all. Below him the stairwell continued its switchback course for several more flights, leading to the basement. It would be completely flooded down there, but maybe he could find another way out before he got that far.

He looked up and was startled to see that the double was only a few steps away. Even at its measured pace, it was overtaking him. Water ran into his eyes, momentarily blinding him. He swiped it away and scrambled down the twisting stairs. He was terrified of losing his grip and falling into the path of the double.

It seemed like an eternity before he finally reached the end. One more flight of stairs would take him into the basement, but the water was several feet deep. Still, he was out of options.

He plunged into icy water up to his waist and pushed his way to the far wall of the basement. Where there was no door. He threw himself at the flat grey surface, pounding it, clawing at it, desperate to find the opening that must be hidden somewhere in the shifting barrier. But there was nothing. Nothing at all.

Behind him he heard the splashing approach of the double and when he whirled round, it was standing right there. Now at last it lowered its pointing finger and the grinning expression melted into a cold, calculating stare.

Allan's legs trembled beneath the water and sank to his knees. The water came up to his neck and he held up his hands to ward off the double.

"Please," he gasped, "I don't know what you want. Don't hurt me. Please let me go. Please…"

But the double ignored his cries, leaning down until it was face to face with him. It pressed its forehead against Allan's. A cold burning sensation swept through him and the water began to rise – horribly and impossibly fast. He struggled, trying to push the double away, but it was as though their heads were fused. He couldn't get to his feet and he had the sudden unpleasant idea that there was nothing left of him beneath the surface of the water. The double seemed unaffected.

The only sound was the relentless splashing as water continued to pour down the stairs, rising to his chin, his mouth, and finally his nose. By then he was too weak to struggle.

His last coherent thought was that he didn't want to die. But as the double continued to absorb him, he realised that this wasn't death. This wasn't even drowning. This was something much worse.

"Allan! Hey mate, what are you doing down here?" It was Simon.

Allan Walker looked up, brushing a few droplets of water from his clothes as the other man clattered down the steps towards him. There was a small puddle outside the door to the basement, but otherwise the stairwell was dry.

"Lord, it stinks in here," Simon said. He touched the wall and grimaced. "Ugh. Can you believe it? Brand new shiny building and it's already acting like a sponge. Anyway, you okay? Anna said she heard screaming coming from the stairwell."

"Yes, I heard that too. It was just a cat that got trapped in here." His lip curled in a faint smile. "It's gone now."

Simon wrinkled his nose at the smell. "Well, you don't want to stay in here. Not if you've got a cold."

He started back up the stairs and Allan

followed at a slower, more measured pace. As he made his way up, he slid his hand along the damp wall. Bringing his fingers to his nose, he inhaled deeply, smiling at the scent. It was salty, almost like tears.

Rapture of the Deep

"He's not worth it," Jo said. It wasn't the first time she'd said it, nor did she suppose it would be the last.

Natalie responded as she did to every iteration of the sentiment – with a weary nod and a look that simultaneously said "I know" and "You're right", but had no real conviction behind it.

Jo shielded her eyes as she looked up into the sky. It was a dazzling blue to match the water, not a single cloud to diminish the scorching glare of the Hawaiian sun. Off in the distance she could just make out the shapes of two sailboats, but otherwise it felt like they had the entire Pacific Ocean to themselves. Surely, with this much distance between them and the continental United States, Natalie could finally start to put that loser Rick out of her mind.

"Are we there yet?"

Jo smiled at her friend's playful tone. At least she was over the endless crying phase. "Almost. I'll go ask Karl." She pushed herself up from the deck and stumbled to her feet, groggy from the heat.

She climbed up to the bridge, where Karl was sitting with his bare feet propped up on the console. "Hey," he said with a lazy wave. "We're nearly there."

"That's what I was just coming to ask you." Jo pushed his feet off the controls and clambered into his lap.

Karl wrapped his muscular arms around her and pressed his lips against the back of her neck. "How's your friend doing?"

Jo shivered a little at the kiss and arched her neck forward so he could continue trailing kisses down her spine. "Oh, she'll be all right. I think. I hope."

"Poor thing," Karl said, his voice muffled against her shoulder. "She seems like a nice girl."

Jo sighed and pulled his arms tighter around herself as she leaned back against his chest. He smelled of sunscreen and seawater. "She is. But she's got an uncanny knack for attracting predators."

Karl laughed. "So you thought you'd show her some *real* sharks."

"Oh, I hadn't thought of it like that!"

"You aren't worried she'll freak out?"

Jo shook her head. "Why would she? They're only hammerheads."

He manoeuvred her around until she was facing him. "I mean the dive. You said she's never done this before."

"She's been snorkelling. I hadn't even done that before I did my first dive."

Karl rolled his eyes. "Your first dive was ten metres down on an easy reef with no current and plenty of fish to look at. A blue water descent is the complete opposite and the absolute worst place for a newbie to start. You're literally throwing her in at the deep end."

"It's the same ocean, whether there's a reef or a shipwreck or nothing at all."

"That's just it. There's nothing at all, only the open sea. Nothing for visual orientation. It even unnerves me and I'm a native."

Jo frowned and drew back, genuinely surprised by his concern. After a moment, she laughed. "And

I always thought *you* were the reckless one! Honestly, I think it's just what she needs to get her mind off things. Nothing short of a life-altering experience is going to snap her out of it."

"Sounded like yesterday was about all the life-altering she could handle," Karl said dubiously.

They both peered over the controls to see Natalie lying on the deck, her limbs splayed as she soaked up the sun. She hadn't enjoyed the previous day's excursion to Maunakea at all. The drive from sea level to the volcano's summit had taken more than two hours, and Natalie had started feeling the effects of altitude sickness well before they reached the observatory at 14,000 feet.

Jo had pushed her, insisting they continue. She'd honestly thought the symptoms would go away once Natalie saw the view from the top. Instead she'd wound up holding Natalie's hair out of her face as the poor girl crouched in the snow to throw up the piña coladas and crab they'd had for lunch. She complained that her head was splitting, that she was dizzy and cold. Jo had tried hard not to feel resentful. It was a long way to go just to glance around for five minutes and then leave. Jo blamed Rick for sending Natalie into such a tailspin that she couldn't cope with the height.

But she'd put her frustrations aside and driven them back down, silently berating herself for being a bad, selfish friend. She'd never experienced mountain sickness herself, so she had no idea what it was like and it wasn't fair to blame Natalie for spoiling the day. But Jo was determined to show her friend as many amazing things as possible during her two-week visit. And an easy dive with hammerhead sharks shouldn't make her sick or freak her out at all, blue water descent or no.

"She'll be fine," Jo said firmly.

Karl still didn't seem convinced. "I hope you're right. Because we're here."

~

Natalie pulled the wetsuit on over her bikini, disliking the sensation of the tight neoprene. She felt smothered, both by the wetsuit and her friend. Jo was trying way too hard to be the ultimate tour guide when all Natalie really wanted to do was chill out in a pretty spot, drink cocktails and read a book.

"It's like a thousand degrees out here," she said, arming sweat off her forehead. "I'm gonna bake in this thing."

"Trust me," Jo said, "you need it. It gets cold down there."

"What if I don't like it and want to come back up?"

"You'll love it, I promise."

Natalie made a face. "You said that yesterday."

"Yeah, well, I'm sorry about that. But you won't get sick this time."

"Okay, then, in the *extremely* unlikely event that I do…"

Jo shrugged. "Then use the safeword and we'll abort the dive."

"What's the safeword?"

"*Humuhumunukunukuapua'a.*"

Natalie blinked, wondering when Jo had suddenly learned to speak Hawaiian. Then she recognised the word. It was the state fish. She rolled her eyes, smiling. "Are you ever serious about anything?"

Jo's expression changed. "Hey, I just want you to have a nice time."

Natalie blushed at Jo's sudden serious

expression. It made her feel sheepish and ungrateful. She wrapped her arms around her friend and squeezed her tightly. "I am," she said. "Really I am. Thank you."

Jo returned the hug forcefully and gave Natalie a sisterly kiss on the cheek. "Don't thank me until you've seen the sharks," she said. Then she pulled away and grabbed the next piece of gear.

Natalie struggled into the buoyancy vest and stood patiently while Jo adjusted the straps and buckles for her. She felt like a horse being saddled. Looking over her friend's shoulder, she suddenly saw something break the surface of the water some distance away. She gasped and gave a little cry.

"What? What is it?" Jo asked, spinning around.

Natalie pointed in the direction she'd seen the movement, but there was nothing there.

"Did you guys see that?" Karl asked excitedly, scrambling down from the bridge. A camera swung from a strap around his neck and he grabbed it before it could smash into the bulkhead.

Natalie turned to him. "See what?"

"Humpback whales! Two, maybe three. Maybe a whole pod. Oh man, now I wish I was going with you. You'll probably hear them singing!"

"Fantastic," Jo exclaimed. "Come on, Nat, let's get in the water!"

Natalie's eyes widened and suddenly she was excited about the dive. She hurriedly strapped her fins on and wound her long blonde hair into a sloppy bun before pulling on her mask. It fogged up instantly and she remembered what Jo had told her. Feeling a little self-conscious, she spat on the lenses and wiped them with her fingers. Then she dipped the mask into the little pail of seawater and shook it off before putting it back on.

Jo was attaching her scuba tank and Karl helped Natalie with hers. Then the three of them ran through an equipment check.

"You're good to go," Karl said.

Natalie nodded, but she couldn't speak with the regulator in her mouth. Jo and Karl each took an arm and helped her stand up. She had never felt so awkward and ungainly in her life. The tank weighed a ton and the fins were like enormous clown shoes. She stumbled towards the back of the boat, imagining how ridiculous she must look.

"Don't worry," Jo said. "Once you're in the water you'll be weightless. This is the worst part, I promise."

Karl held onto Natalie's shoulders to keep her from falling over as her friend edged past her. Jo put her regulator back in and pressed one hand against it and her mask, then stretched out one foot and took a giant step off the boat. After a moment's submersion she bobbed to the surface and gave the "okay" signal.

"Your turn," Karl said.

Natalie felt her heart lurch with momentary panic as Karl released her, but then she saw a huge grey shape off in the distance. It surged up out of the water and she stared in awe as the whale breached, turning sideways, its white flukes and streamlined belly shining in the sun. She could almost believe it was waving at her. It hung in the air for what seemed like whole minutes before falling once more into the ocean with a great splash. Dimly she registered the clicking of Karl's camera beside her.

Down in the water, Jo was cheering. "Oh my god, did you see that? That was incredible! Nat, come on, get in here, jump!"

Smiling around her regulator, Natalie didn't

need any further encouragement. She copied what Jo had done and felt instantly refreshed as she plunged into the cool water. Once she surfaced again, Jo made an adjustment to her mask strap for her and then fussed with her buoyancy controls for a moment before giving her the "okay" signal with a questioning expression.

Natalie nodded and returned the gesture. They both looked up at Karl, who was waving to them. Jo gave a thumbs-down signal and deflated her vest, sinking out of sight. Natalie felt a flutter of unease as she imagined a Roman emperor giving that same signal. But then she thought of the whale and pushed the fear aside. Once more she copied Jo's actions and found herself sinking as well. The water closed over her head.

For a few seconds she just floated there, staring around her. There was nothing to see. Nothing but blue. Endless blue in all directions. Above her was a wavering carpet of light, their only way out, and it was receding. Everything else was ocean. She might as well be floating in outer space. The horrible vertigo she'd experienced on Maunakea was returning. The immensity of the unfamiliar world she was in threatened to overwhelm her and her heart began to gallop as she turned left and right frantically, terrified to realise that she'd lost sight of Jo.

But her friend was right there. She grabbed Natalie's arm as she pointed to her own regulator. Behind the mask, Jo's eyes were wide. She began miming something urgently and Natalie finally caught on. She took a breath.

The sensation was bizarre and comforting in equal measure, and the enriched air banished the dizziness instantly. Natalie felt a surge of exhilaration. She was breathing underwater! She exhaled and watched her bubbles scurry up towards the light.

Jo signalled a question and Natalie responded. OKAY. Then she made the same sign with her other hand, for emphasis. She was more than okay. She had forgotten the awful altitude sickness, the heat, the heartbreak. She'd forgotten everything but the present moment. This was where she was meant to be.

Jo did a little victory dance in the water and gestured for Natalie to follow her. After a few kicks, Natalie saw the anchor line. They both took hold of it and then Jo began moving down, climbing hand-over-hand along the rope, heading into the inky depths below. Natalie followed her.

She was still trying to adjust to the strange environment when she heard an even stranger sound. A haunting low note, alien and beautiful. For a moment she forgot to breathe, then remembered Jo warning her earlier not to hold her breath. Her lungs could burst. She slowed her breathing instead, trying to make as little noise as possible so she could hear the whalesong.

When the pressure built up in her ears, she pinched her nose and blew to equalise it. Immediately the whalesong grew louder. She stopped where she was on the rope and looked up. The boat was only a vague blur, dark against the flickering light. It looked like a leaf floating in a pool. Natalie looked all around her for the whales, but there was nothing to see. For a moment she felt disorientated, uncertain which direction she was facing. But a sudden tapping noise made her look down. Jo was there, knocking on her tank with a metal carabiner and signing to her. Checking on her.

OKAY, Natalie signed back, and resumed her descent. This time Jo gestured for her go ahead of her and Natalie did, pulling herself along the rope. It disappeared into the darkness, as though it might go on forever. But she reminded herself that the anchor was down there somewhere. They would come to it eventually.

The whales were singing all around them like a ghostly choir and at last fish began to appear. Large toothy silver ones with long snouts and smaller brightly coloured ones in bizarre triangular shapes. She wondered if one of them was the amusingly-named *Humuhumunukunukuapua'a*.

Safeword, she thought with a smile. *Good one, Jo.* How the hell was she supposed to speak down here? Divers in movies always did, but she hadn't even thought about her mouth being gagged with the cumbersome regulator. But the deeper she went, the more she realised that it wouldn't be necessary. Jo was right. She did love it.

~

Jo watched Natalie carefully as they descended the anchor line. At the same time she kept a lookout for whales and other creatures. She'd often seen sea turtles out here. She spotted a few barracuda and the usual triggerfish, but if there were hammerheads around, they would be lower still.

She checked her depth gauge and saw they had almost reached thirty metres. She wasn't taking Natalie any deeper than forty. There was nothing like having to make a boring decompression stop to spoil the mood of a great dive.

From every direction came the song of humpback whales and Jo closed her eyes for a while just to listen. To human ears, their music sounded mournful and melancholy. But perhaps it was how whales expressed joy. There was no way to know. Scientists had all sorts of theories as to why they sang. To attract mates. To help with migration. Jo preferred to think they sang for the same reason humans did – for the sheer pleasure of it. Maybe they were love songs. Or prayers. Or maybe they were epic ballads, telling and retelling the adventures of great whale heroes down through the ages.

She could actually feel the vibrations of their voices through the water, resonating deep into her bones. It was like being inside the song itself. But no matter how hard she peered into the blue, she could not see the whales.

Jo carried on down the anchor line, continually scanning the area around them. And then she spotted the telltale shapes of hammerhead sharks. Karl was an expert at tracking down the shyest and most secretive of animals and he'd really come through today. She grabbed Natalie's fin to halt her descent. Her friend jerked, startled, until she saw it was only Jo. Pointing, Jo directed her attention to the object of their quest.

There were several, all circling below them in a lazy orbit around a school of small silvery fish. Jo counted at least seven sharks before realising there were even more beneath those.

Native Hawaiian belief held that sharks were gods of the ocean, and hammerheads were especially revered. Karl said they were *aumakua*, deified ancestors. Jo couldn't help but wonder if any of the ones swimming beneath her now were inhabited by the spirits of Karl's family.

It was such a strange and beautiful thing to believe, far more comforting than the idea of heaven. Jo liked the idea of returning as an animal to watch over her loved ones. Although, given the choice, she'd rather come back as a whale. Then she would know for sure why they sang.

She touched her fingertips to her regulator and blew a bubbly kiss to Karl up above, thanking him for finding this place.

When she looked back down towards the sharks, she froze. Natalie was gone.

~

The ocean was alive with whale music and Natalie was transfixed by the circling sharks. She had never seen stranger animals in her life. They moved with a strange mechanical grace, their flattened heads swaying from side to side as they swam. They didn't resemble hammers so much as wings, with the eyes at either distant tip. What did the world look like through eyes positioned like that? Could they see in all directions at once?

The sharks fanned out, herding the smaller fish into the centre of their spiral before darting in to snap them up. Then they swam out and back in again. And again. As though they were dancing. Natalie felt herself being drawn down into the maelstrom of flickering bodies. She was barely even aware of her hands dragging her along the rope. But she still didn't seem to be getting any closer to the sharks.

It felt like she was simply holding the rope and someone far down below was pulling on it, reeling her in. She envisioned another diver down there, waiting to surprise them. Maybe Karl had jumped in after all and reached the bottom before them.

Natalie squinted through the mask and now she was convinced she saw a pair of muscular arms hauling on the rope. At first she took the dark, jagged marks encircling them for seaweed. Then she realised they must be tribal tattoos. Karl did have quite a few.

He must be down by the anchor. She wondered how deep it was. Jo had shown her how to check her depth gauge, and Natalie realised suddenly that she hadn't even looked at it once. Well, Jo would have been checking hers anyway, controlling every aspect of the dive. And Karl wouldn't be dragging her into deeper water than she could handle.

The sharks continued their spiralling dance, swimming through the water between Natalie and Karl. Each shark left a shimmering trail behind it, like a ghostly wake. Natalie stared hard, convinced they were forming words. But try as she might, she couldn't read the messages.

The whalesong filled her head as she hung on the rope, captivated by the music and the dance as she was drawn deeper and deeper into both.

~

Jo pawed at her buoyancy vest, her hands shaking as she fumbled for the metal carabiner. She unclipped it and reached behind her to knock it against her tank, hoping Natalie would hear it and be able to find her. But a sudden lurch yanked the rope out of her hand, and as she grabbed for it again, she dropped the carabiner. It plummeted out of sight.

She pulled her depth gauge up to her face and swore silently. Forty-seven metres. They were beyond the safety range, for both decompression and nitrogen narcosis.

Natalie must have been so mesmerised by the sharks that she just kept following them deeper and deeper. And now Jo had no choice but to go after her.

~

Something sailed past Natalie's head. She thought it was a tiny fish until she realised it was metal. A little oblong loop, like a link from a chain. She reached out for it as it fell, but she wasn't quick enough to grab it. It tumbled through the water, turning end over end. Maybe it was a fish after all. It seemed to be beckoning her.

She let go of the rope and kicked her legs, diving into the shadowy depths, following the little metallic fish. The sharks parted for her, opening like a gate to let her in. She glided into the spiral and hovered in their midst, utterly spellbound. She might be on another planet, surrounded by aliens.

Her hand moved by itself, reaching out to the sharks. One sleek silvery body slid past and she ran her fingers along its length as though stroking a cat. Were they responding to the whalesong? Sharks didn't sing, but maybe they listened. Maybe all the creatures of the ocean listened.

She had almost forgotten about Karl. She looked for the rope, but she could no longer see it. In some distant, rational part of her mind, a logical conundrum presented itself: if Karl really had been pulling the rope to draw her down to the sea bed, where was the boat? With a sense of disquiet, she realised that she had no idea where she was. All around her the sharks swam in dizzying corkscrew patterns, none of them remaining upright or stationary for long.

Natalie began to panic as the disorientation of the open sea took hold. It was like when she had first jumped into the water. There was nothing to focus on, nothing to give her a fix on where she was or which direction was up. She couldn't even rely on gravity any more. Down here she was weightless. Where was the sky? To the side? Above? Below?

She spun around, searching in every direction, but all she could see were the sharks, slicing through the water, surrounding her. Their movements seemed different now, deliberate. If they had seemed to be dancing before, now there was something even stranger in their display. It was mystifying and yet somehow oddly familiar. And as she watched them, she began to make connections in her mind, connections with the distant past. And she finally understood what she was seeing. The whalesong changed key, dropping lower, the notes becoming more solemn. She was witnessing was a ritual.

Natalie closed her eyes and took a slow, deep inhalation, breathing the music. She could feel the sensual texture of each lingering tone, the ancient force behind the song. It was the voice of the ocean and everything within it.

When she opened her eyes, she knew exactly where she wanted to go. She spun in a circle and aimed for the centre of the sharks. She laid her arms back along her body and pressed her legs together, streamlining herself like a whale as she propelled herself into their midst.

The rope was there, thick and ancient and crusted with barnacles. She kept her hands at her sides and didn't reach for it. Instead she kept going down, heading for the bottom, for whatever was calling to her.

~

Jo caught a glimpse of Natalie just before she vanished into the murk. She had been playing with the sharks, dancing with them. She had the disturbing thought that Natalie had been trying to talk to them. Jo's stomach plunged as she realised the danger they were both in. Her friend was definitely narked. She might be terrified or euphoric, hallucinating or blind. Jo could only hope she didn't stray too far from the anchor line. If she followed it to the bottom, to where the anchor lay, she might realise where she was and come to her senses enough to stay where Jo could find her.

Jo checked her air. She still had plenty, but Natalie wouldn't know to conserve hers for such a deep dive. They needed air for the decompression stop they'd have to do. Jo tried to do the calculations in her head, tried to think how long they'd have to wait before they could ascend, but she was finding it hard to concentrate herself. It all depended on how deep they ended up going, and how long they were trapped there. Her depth gauge showed she'd just passed the fifty metre mark and Natalie was still nowhere in sight. Tears stung her eyes.

~

The rope led Natalie deeper and deeper, stretching away into the empty vastness of the sea. She swam with a whale's undulating up-

and-down motion, her legs pressed together, the fins on her feet acting like the flukes of a tail to propel her. She began to circle the rope, spiralling around it as the sharks had. The hammerheads were still with her, following her, guiding her.

Then she saw a figure in the distance. A tiny spindly form was emerging from the darkness. Something in its awkward configuration of limbs was familiar and for a moment Natalie's mind cleared. The whalesong gave way to an odd sound. A harsh, discordant note. A name. Jo.

~

Jo was on the verge of panic when at last she saw the unmistakable silhouette of a diver. She kicked harder, putting on a burst of speed to reach Natalie before she vanished again. She was startled to see that Natalie appeared to be moving upwards, moving towards her. Maybe she'd lost all sense of up or down and had finally realised how to get to the surface. Jo was no longer sure herself which direction was which. She signalled to Natalie, trying to get her to slow her ascent. If she came up too fast, she'd give herself the bends.

Bubbles streamed away from the figure and Natalie saw it was waving frantically, like a fish in distress. She swam towards it and around it. The sound came again inside her head. Jo. The sound that was a name.

Natalie circled her, avoiding the grasping arms that reached for her. Fear came off Jo in violent pulses and Natalie had to dart away so as not to be caught. Could she not hear the song? Why would she not join the dance?

~

Jo stared at her friend in horror. She was swimming in a bizarre manner, with her arms pinned to her sides and her legs pressed together. Even so, she moved with breathtaking speed. The sharks had come up with her. They swam around her in dizzying coils and loops, as though Natalie was the nucleus of some great source of energy and they were feeding off her.

~

Natalie swam away and turned, then powered towards Jo, ramming her head into Jo's body, stunning her as a shark might. Jo went limp and Natalie nosed against her, pushing her down, pushing her deeper.

~

Jo was dazed, but she could feel herself being driven downwards. But the water was all wrong. Even through her wetsuit, it abraded her skin, burning her. Her bones ached from the vibration of the whalesong. It was deafening.

She looked around her, but there was nothing to see but the blue. And the sharks. The strange, alien sharks. *Aumakua*, she thought. What were they really? Ghosts? Gods?

Behind her mask, her eyes streamed with tears, blurring her vision. She struggled against the pressure of the water, but Natalie was too strong. The descent was relentless.

Helpless, she watched the dancing sharks. There was something ecstatic in their movements, something ancient and primal. If they were gods, they wanted prayers. And the songs of the whales were no longer enough. Jo's thoughts were clouding, but strange images came to her. Wild tribal dances and frenzied singing. Rituals. Offerings. Sacrifice.

A chill pierced her heart.

A ritual required a priest. And a sacrifice required a victim. The sharks had chosen Natalie. And Natalie had chosen Jo.

She fought against the current, struggling to push away from Natalie, but the water was tearing her skin apart. A cloud of dark blood streamed out behind her as her bubbles came to an abrupt end. There was no more air. Natalie's air must have run out too but she was still swimming, guided by the sharks darting all around her.

Jo's mind began to crack. Her mask had disintegrated, but her failing eyesight granted her one last vision. The water surrounding her was alive. She could see each single molecule, a bubble with two smaller bubbles swelling outwards from its centre. Each one was both eye and mouth, opening wide. Seeing her, devouring her.

As her awareness faded, she heard Natalie begin to sing.

"How inappropriate to call this planet Earth when it is quite clearly Ocean."

- Arthur C Clarke

The kettle hissed, its dragon-breath steaming, like fire reborn as water.

Tara poured the boiling contents into the teapot, inhaling the salty aroma of the seaweed tea. The box claimed all sorts of "benefits" of drinking it, but Tara had no interest in feeble magic promises. She just wanted to drink the ocean.

There was a strange poetry in the fact that seawater was poisonous to drink. Such irony to know that you could die from dehydration whilst consuming water. The human body was half water, after all, and salt. We were practically made of sea. But within that body, our fragile little kidneys were too weak to filter such concentrated amounts of salt from the wider ocean.

Two things you needed to survive: water and salt. And together they could kill you.

The tea tasted sharp and slightly bitter, but pleasantly so. It made Tara think of sushi and Japanese spices. It made her feel calm.

She returned to the hothouse of the bathroom, swirling the steam with her passage. The water was perfect, just shy of scalding. The bath salts made it smell like the sea. A torrent rushed from the hot tap, and only a trickle from the cold. She turned them both off and dipped a cautious toe into the tub.

It was so hot it felt cold, and she thought of climbers driven mad by the mountains they wanted to conquer. She'd heard stories of people stripping off their clothes at dangerous altitudes, believing themselves to be burning up instead of freezing. The brutality of snow and ice. Whatever form it took, it was still only water. Essential, deadly water.

She knew all the numbers. Water covered 71% of the planet's surface, and a staggering 96.5% of it was seawater. Even more fascinating was the fact that three-quarters of the remaining freshwater was ice. So little of it was accessible to humans, so little of it safe. And with the ice caps melting and the seas rising, soon there might be no more fresh water at all, only the immense ocean, hostile and undrinkable.

Tara had managed to submerge one foot, gradually lowering it deeper into the tub. The foot turned bright red beneath the steaming surface, like a soft, fleshy lobster.

She entered a bath the way a tentative swimmer entered a pool, inch by slow wincing inch. It took time, but eventually she was able to sit down, hissing with pain as the water sloshed higher up her skin than she was prepared for.

When at last she was able to lie back, she sipped her tea, envisioning its liquid journey through her insides. Water within and without, separated only by the thin veil of her flesh.

As a child, she'd been told that human skin acted like a sponge in water, slowly absorbing it, and that if you stayed in the bath too long, you could absorb enough water to drown. She'd never been brave enough to test the theory back then, and even now that she knew it wasn't true, she still couldn't help but keep an eye on the water level, watching to see if it would go down.

Lies told to children died hard.

She dozed off, waking to find that the water had cooled considerably. Her toes sought the handle of the hot tap at the foot of the bath. One solemn droplet leaked out every few seconds from the cold one, hitting the steaming surface of the water with a small splash. It was kind of sad, the idea that these little beads of cold were instantly lost in the sea of hot. She gripped the handle with her feet, twisting it anticlockwise to send another torrent rushing into the bath. The pipes groaned when she turned it off.

She positioned her big toe beneath the cold tap and felt the droplet slide down the length of her foot and across her instep, where it vanished. She arched her foot beneath it to encourage a steady trickle. It felt like a long cold spill of jelly racing along her shin. Like a chilly finger. Like the icy tongue of something that lived inside the pipes.

The image was unwelcome, disturbing. She felt chilled in spite of the scalding bath. The back of her neck prickled and she rubbed it until the sensation went away.

The heat was making her light-headed. Unless it was the water. Maybe her skin really was soaking it up. Was her brain filling with water? She imagined droplets scurrying all along the maze of tissue, seeping inside, turning the grey matter into mush, like soggy bread inside her skull.

The thought of it made her feel queasy and she pushed herself up with a splash, sloshing water over the side. And froze. Something was wrong.

The sound of the water had seemed delayed, like an echo of her movement. She listened, but there was nothing else to hear. Only the persistent *plink* of the droplet from the cold tap.

Tara pulled the plug and the bath began its long throaty gurgle as it drank the water she had been lying in, swallowing sloughs of skin and hair, consuming the parts of her she left behind.

She stepped out, placing her feet carefully on the mat to leave a pleasing pattern of footprints behind. The soft cotton towel felt rough against her skin, like a cat's tongue. The sultry, steamy air of the bathroom wasn't warm enough to keep the chill from returning and soon she was shivering again. Even her flannel pyjamas burned, as though she'd shaved over gooseflesh.

The bedroom was cold, and she tucked the hot water bottle under the duvet to warm the sheets while she checked and re-checked that the front door was locked. When she was satisfied that nothing could get in, she crawled into bed to stare at the shape on the wall until an uneasy sleep claimed her and she had the dream again.

She saw dolphins. Strange prehistoric ones. They crawled on legs that were somewhere between hands and flippers. But they didn't like the gravity-bound life of creatures that could neither swim nor fly. They gazed longingly out at the endless blue expanse of water and the waves called to them in seductive hissing whispers.

Come closer, they said. *Come inside. We will enfold you in liquid sleep and you will wake into magnificence.*

The dolphins crept into the water.

They danced beneath and above the waves, having made their choice. The millions of years it had taken was a luxury mankind did not have. His time was running out.

Man was of the hopelessly naive impression that he had damaged the planet, that he, with all his tiny industry and tiny wars, had somehow caused irreparable harm. He pointed to his intelligence as proof of his superiority over all other creatures, including the Earth itself. But it was that very intelligence that would be the downfall of his own species.

The dolphins had chosen, but theirs was an instinctive choice. They were in tune with their surroundings. They heard the voice of the ocean and followed it, while mankind believed it was his to control. But the water was creeping in, drop by drop, slowly and inexorably reclaiming the planet. Soon 71% would become 72. Then 73. And so on.

Tara wasn't sure where the dream ended and reality began. It was the same dream she'd been having since she was little, when she'd believed that raindrops were the fingers of the sea. The water would have its day, she'd been told. It came from above and below, and any creatures not suited for survival in its depths would perish.

When she woke, she looked up at the wall. Even in the pale morning light, she could see that the stain had grown. Each day it was a little larger, a little more splayed. A little more like a grasping hand. It was the hand of something that had emerged from the aquatic world just long enough to explore the land. Long enough to decide that whatever lived there would not be there long.

Tara had once lain awake all night with the light on, paralysed by the sight of the wood grain striations in the door of her wardrobe, convinced that they were the long, insectoid legs of a monster that lived inside the door. It was waiting, and it would slip out of the flat world and into the round one as soon as she looked away.

The stain on the wall had the same effect on her now. She'd watched it grow from a little smudge into the sprawling blotch it was now. There had been similar blotches on the walls of her childhood home. Her mother had called them fingerprints, and Tara had been too afraid to ask whose hands had made them. Water took so many forms: sea, rain, snow, ice. Which of them had tried to claw apart the house?

Rising damp was the explanation given by the estate agent when Tara had put the house up for sale, a term she found curious. She envisioned something wet and insubstantial living beneath the foundation, something gradually rising up through the walls, seeping into the rooms. Water was life; therefore water was alive.

Every morning it was the same. She woke tangled in the sticky web of dreams and memories, unable to distinguish one from the other. Had she really once seen the living past, heard the voice of the ocean like laughter as it welcomed the dolphins?

She made more seaweed tea, filling the kitchen with the salty aroma of bladderwrack. She'd heard about poisoners building up an immunity to arsenic so they could share it with their victims, killing them whilst being unaffected themselves. Was it possible to do the same with seawater? Could the human body be trained to handle ever greater amounts of salt? Could one force evolution?

Tara looked into her mug. The hand that held it was still human. Spindly and fragile. It had not changed in the night. She often dreamed she would be different when she woke, but each morning her hands looked the same.

Dolphins had finger bones inside their pectoral fins, proof that they had once walked on earth. How long would Tara's own finger bones last once she had changed? Mankind would have to evolve if he was to survive, would have to learn to embrace the wide, wet world when it finally consumed the land. He had come from the ocean. Perhaps he never should have left it.

Mount Everest had once been under water, the towering Himalayas forced upward by the collision of continents. One day they would be submerged again, along with everything else. The land would sink.

She'd heard that drowning was a peaceful, painless death. That it was like coming home. Tara pictured it often, wondered how it would feel to breathe the water in, to fill her lungs with it. She imagined it would be like the warm passage of tea down her throat and into her stomach, soothing and comforting. She tried not to fear it.

But there were those the water did not love. There were those it haunted.

She thought of the little Zen garden she'd given Daniel. Such a calming act, combing the soft sand with the tiny wooden rake, forming swirls to position the stones among. She had hoped it would calm him too. But one day the sand changed, became like that on the seashore, hard-packed and wet. It clogged the fingers of the rake and stuck to the stones. *I'm coming*, the water seemed to say.

Not long after that, she'd noticed the pictures. They were stained and smelly, curling up from the pages of the photo album. So many smiling faces soaked with damp, like a wedding on a sunken ship.

The water was coming through.

She finished her tea, finished her communion with the ocean. She drank its blood as it would one day drink hers. As she padded back to the bedroom, she noticed something odd about the floor. It felt soft, spongy. Looking down, she saw that it was wet. Her bare feet were splashing through thin puddles across the wooden floor.

"Is it time?" she asked, her voice ringing in the flooded hallway.

But the water gave no reply. It lay in small, still pools, rippling only where she disturbed it with her feet. The floorboards were warped and twisted, smelling of the damp. The estate agent had told her she'd need to have them fixed or the house would never sell. But Tara wasn't even sure she wanted to sell it now. Little pockets of algae were beginning to sprout from the edges of the pools, new life blossoming inside her home. Who was she to say it didn't belong there?

Her feet squished in the bedroom carpet. It had been dry the night before. Had it rained? Had the roof leaked? Surely that was the most obvious place for the water to get in. Listening, she caught the sound of a drip, the soft, musical *plink* of a single droplet. But it wasn't raining. It hadn't rained for days.

The damp carpet was cold beneath her feet, and she pulled her dressing gown tight as she crossed to the bathroom. And she froze when she heard the voice.

She couldn't make out the whispered words, but soon there came an answering gurgle, a guttural rumble. Her skin crawled and she stood listening before the closed door for several minutes. Then at last she sagged with relief. The pipes. It was only the water.

She pushed open the door and stepped inside. The cold tap was dripping slowly but steadily into the tub, splashing in the standing water. But that was odd. She was sure she'd drained it the night before. As if in answer to her confusion, the pipes gave a hoarse rattle and the hot tap spat forth a spurt of greenish water.

Had she only dreamed the bath? Or had she filled the tub in a trance and slipped into its watery embrace while asleep?

Was she still dreaming now?

She looked down at the bath mat and saw the wet footprints she had left. And frowned. They weren't right. They were far too large for a start – swollen and bloated. Crouching down for a closer look, she noticed that the webbing between the toes seemed more pronounced. Yet her own toes and fingers looked normal enough.

Unnerved, she plunged her hand into the bath and pulled the chain to unstopper it. The pipes roared as the level began to go down and she watched until the tiny maelstrom appeared, pulling all the liquid back down into the maze of pipes beneath the house.

She remembered Daniel crawling under there once, remembered him banging on the pipes while she shouted back the results of his actions. But that was a long time ago. The only thing that made the pipes bang now was the water rushing through them.

Her eyes turned back to the bath mat, to the

damp footprints there. Her hand was still wet and she pressed it into a dry part of the material. The resulting print looked as normal as the hand that had made it.

With a shrug, she got to her feet and turned to go. A sudden sound stopped her in her tracks. A splash. But when she looked back at the tub, there was nothing there. Nothing but water swirling down the drain. It had sounded exactly like the delayed sloshing she'd heard the night before. Maybe the water *had* got to her brain. Or maybe the seawater tea was beginning to transform her at last.

She looked down at the bath mat again and her eyes widened. The handprint had changed. Just like the footprints, it too had more pronounced webbing between the digits. But her hand still looked perfectly normal.

All at once Tara felt dizzy. She backed away, edging into the bedroom, where her bare feet encountered more water in the sodden carpet. It was cold, and the chill penetrated her instantly as the level rose to her ankles. Looking down, she saw bits of green floating in it and at first she thought they were leaves. But as one long strand entangled itself around her leg she realised it was seaweed.

The water was rising. Before long it had reached her knees. A salty, pungent smell permeated the house.

On the wall, the stain had changed. It no longer resembled a hand, but something that had once *been* a hand. Something that had chosen another form. The dampness bulged out from the wall, filling the wallpaper like a balloon. Soon it would burst.

Tara stared at it in fascination. Within her body, her heart hammered madly, in terror. Yet she felt none of the actual fear herself. It seemed like a distant memory. She heard splashing, wild and frantic, a screaming voice. She saw a face with bulging eyes, a gasping mouth, clutching hands. Water churned and frothed and then the face was gone, sinking slowly below the surface.

The water had come for her at last.

The level rose to her hips as she reached up to the swollen pocket on the wall. A line of dots appeared, four sharp spiny points pressing outward. Tara touched her fingers to them as they punctured the wallpaper, sending forth a torrent of green, astringent water. It poured over her face. It tasted like tea.

An arm reached for her, long and strange and

splayed. It looked like bone, ancient and yellow, tufted with clots of algae. As the pouring water passed over it, the algae grew, spreading rapidly to cover the skeletal appendage like skin.

Tara clutched at it, noticing as she did that her own arm was darkening, turning green. Now the webbing between her fingers was starting to show. She could hear squelching sounds from the bathroom, the movements of something else coming through. She closed her eyes and found she could see it, pressing up from the prints on the bathmat as its companion emerged from the wall. The water had colonised her brain. It was alive and taking hold.

Once again she heard the echo, the delayed splash that had disturbed her. She thought she heard a voice. It was familiar, but altered. Distorted like the sand in the Zen garden, like the photographs in the wedding album.

The wall crumbled against the weight of the creature pushing through. It fell on her, forcing her under the water. She cried out but there was no sound. Her eyes flew open and she gazed in wonder at her submerged surroundings. The waves must have engulfed the entire house, sinking it. The surface seemed so far away and it was growing more distant with each second. Yet she felt no fear.

Before her the creature floated, waving its fins as it hung in the water, its eyes meeting hers. She could see perfectly. And she watched as the webbing stretched between her fingers, spreading her hands wider and wider. Her legs had stopped kicking and she realised they were fused together. Her feet were undergoing the same transformation.

With a flick of her tail she turned in the water, her movements fluid and effortless. She swam through the arch of the doorway, through the sunken ruin of the house.

The bathroom alone remained dry, isolated in its own bubble of air and terrestrial gravity. She floated at the vertical edge of the water in the doorway, the border she could not cross.

Inside, something was still emerging from the mat, materialising from the damp footprints. She heard the echoing slosh of water in the bath and registered the figure lying in it. There was something familiar about the face, but she found her thoughts becoming too abstract to distinguish the features. But his eyes were wide with terror as he saw the shape of what rose before him from the floor.

The bloated, decomposing shape was hung with seaweed, and green tendrils trailed behind it as it drifted above him, floating in water he could not see, water that was no part of his world. He screamed and covered his eyes, sobbing and murmuring apologies, regrets. Confessions. But the shape was unmoved, unaffected either by his terror or his remorse. His world could no longer touch hers.

But she could touch his.

Her body had never been found. Not by those who sought justice for what he had done to her. But death was not the end. It was only a step. She had known it was coming and she had prepared herself for it. She had been ready to transform.

Behind her other creatures were emerging from the wall, the strange dolphins she'd been seeing all her life. They were real. They were calling to her. They had made her one of them.

The last lingering image of her former state would remain to haunt the man who had drowned her. It would inhabit every drop of water he encountered. It would seep through the walls, staining everything it touched. The world was changing, but he would never change in time to be a part of it. She alone had been chosen.

She was aware of a sense of satisfaction, of pleasure, before the thoughts dissolved like salt into water and she turned with her companions to swim into the wider ocean, the ocean that now entirely covered the surface of the planet.

Story Notes

This collection went through a lot of title changes. Originally it was going to be called *Dark and Lonely Water*, after the infamous public information film with Donald Pleasence as Death. And originally one of the stories was going to have that title as well. But these things almost never go according to plan. I have John Llewellyn Probert to thank for the actual title.

About the only thing that did go as planned was the theme. When Steve Shaw asked for a micro-collection of connected stories, the first theme that came to me was water. It's a strange thing. I'm not afraid of water at all and in fact, I feel very much at home in it (assuming it's warm!). From the first moment I tried scuba diving, I felt as though I belonged down there, floating weightless among the sea life. The ocean fascinates me. I feel like water is my natural element.

And yet I'm compelled to write stories where water is dangerous or evil, or harbouring something that is. Well, I'm not afraid of it, but plenty of people are. So if you're one of them, I hope these stories gave you a little trickle of unease. I say "gave" because I do hope you aren't reading this bit first! If you are, shame on you. (That's all the spoiler warning you're getting.)

~

To Drown the World

Can you tell I'm a little obsessed with the idea of a drowned Earth?

I had just written a story called "Octoberland", set in Houston, where I grew up. It reawakened so many memories and feelings and, while dark, was an extremely nostalgic writing experience. I wanted to explore those feelings again with another place from my childhood – Galveston. I was reminiscing about it with my brother and he told me about a recurring nightmare he used to have about the causeway. It became Evan's nightmare in the story.

This was a strange and difficult one to write because it just kept trying to derail me. My original idea was much simpler (and shorter!) than the story it eventually became. It was just going to be Evan having a premonition of death on the causeway. His car would go in the water and he would see a creature down there, a kind of oil-slick mermaid, slimy black and rainbow-sheened. Lea was perfectly normal. There were no sea-monkeys or apocalyptic overtones.

But wow, my head had other ideas!

I still don't know where some of it came from. I was strolling down Memory Lane (.com) one day and I happened to look up sea-monkeys. I remembered that they were actually just brine shrimp, but I'd never heard the term "cryptobiosis" before. I loved it, and Lea's paper became "Cryptobiosis and the Drowned World". Before I knew it, she had a tank of sea-monkeys to show Evan. I'd already written the crab communion, so that was a natural progression. Climate change is the new nuclear waste as a trigger for eco-horror, so the paper title got changed to "The Poisoned Wellspring: The Real Impact of Climate Change on the Ocean". The little creatures had taken over the story and were now centre stage. And Lea was now insane. But I still wanted to get my original mermaid idea in there, and make Evan's premonition come true. Maybe Lea was always destined to be the mermaid.

~

The Reflection

I had never written a *doppelgänger* story before but I liked the idea of a reflection in water having its own identity. Or rather – stealing the identity of the person it belonged to.

The image of the advancing figure, pointing and grinning, is from a nightmare I had once. The dream figure followed me just like that, backing me up a flight of stairs and when I got to the top of the stairwell I realised there was nowhere to go but the roof.

Water may not scare me, but the idea of losing my identity does.

~

Rapture of the Deep

I really miss diving. I haven't done it in years, but I still remember the sensation. And I couldn't believe I'd only ever written one dive story ("The Curtain"). That one took an unexpectedly Lovecraftian turn, which I was determined to resist this time. Now that I think of it, I've actually written two dive stories. The other one is called "Into Something Rich and Strange", and it's SF, set on an entirely aquatic planet, with futuristic scuba gear.

Loads of people, even experienced divers, find blue water descents unnerving, but I never did. There are plenty of things in the world that scare me, but diving isn't one of them. It's always made me feel calm, like I belonged down there.

I did have one traumatic experience on a dive, but it had nothing to do with the dive itself. It was the fault of the dodgy boat operator in Sharm-el-Sheikh. With a propeller on the rear of the boat, once the divers have splashed in, the boat should move away in reverse. This one didn't and I found myself being pulled towards the churning blades as the boat headed straight for us, ready to plough through all the divers just beneath the surface. Suddenly I was in the Fizzy Lifting scene from the original Willy Wonka movie. I kept drifting closer and closer to the propeller. I didn't dare turn around and try to swim away; I was terrified that my fins would get caught in the blades. Once I got close enough I was able to push against the hull of the boat just ahead of the propeller. That's about when the boat finally stopped and went into reverse. I relived the whole thing again and again all throughout the dive and in every dream for weeks afterwards.

Natalie's experience with the hammerhead sharks happened to me, although I didn't go deep enough to get narked. I was mesmerised by their circling below me and I just kept dropping lower and lower to see them, but never getting any closer. I didn't realise they were dropping too! I did finally hear the bang of carabiner on tank and realised I'd gone beyond 40 metres. Oops. I was also lucky enough to hear humpback whales singing once while diving in Hawaii, although I never got to see them breach. Ah, someday...

~

Where the Water Comes In

Things I fantasised about growing up to be when I was a kid included professional mermaid and marine biologist. Mostly because I love dolphins. I was always fascinated by the idea that, although they came from the water, after a few million years on land, they returned to the sea.

This is a title that had been in the Bradbury Box for years. There was no idea or even image that came with it, just the phrase. One night I dreamt I was in a derelict hospital. But there were still patients there, lying in a circle on the uneven stone floor in a dripping room. That was the image I tried to build on, but it never even made it into the story. Instead, I went into my narrator's head and found a completely different obsession.

Tara's memory of staring at the insectoid legs in the wood grain of the closet door? That was what I spent the entire night staring at after seeing *Alien* at age 8. And yeah, that's exactly how I like my baths too. Borderline scalding. But I'm actually more of a shower person.

There's a lot going on in this story but, like "To Drown the World", it was never meant to be as complicated as that. I really just wanted to write a ghost story where the ghost didn't realise that *they* were the one doing the haunting. But my narrator insisted on obsessing about water statistics and the rising seas, so that found its way in there too.

The damp stains came from an unfinished story and so did the water-slosh echo. There's a stew of loose ideas swimming around in all our heads, and I suppose whatever it is that makes us write just picks and chooses which will fit a given story at a given time. Hey, however it works, at least it works!

~

It's been a blast for me to devote a whole book to my aquaphilia and I hope you've enjoyed the result.

I'm eternally grateful to Steve Shaw for allowing me to indulge myself. Long may Black Shuck reign!

I also owe a debt of gratitude to my brother jesse, who reads all my stuff and lets me pick his brain. Valar Dohaeris, brother! ;-)

And most of all, John, my love and my life. Thank you for being you, always.

Also by Thana Niveau:

Novels

The House of Screaming Death (Horrific Tales, 2018)

Collections

From Hell to Eternity (Gray Friar Press, 2012)
Octoberland (PS Publishing, 2018)

Visit Thana Niveau at her website:
thananiveau.com

*Now available and forthcoming from
Black Shuck Shadows:*

Shadows 1 – The Spirits of Christmas

by Paul Kane

Shadows 2 – Tales of New Mexico

by Joseph D'Lacey

Shadows 3 – Unquiet Waters

by Thana Niveau

Shadows 4 – The Life Cycle

by Paul Kane

Shadows 5 – The Death of Boys

by Gary Fry

Shadows 6 – Broken on the Inside

by Phil Sloman

Shadows 7 – The Martledge Variations

by Simon Kurt Unsworth

Shadows 8 – Singing Back the Dark

by Simon Bestwick

Shadows 9 – Winter Freits
by Andrew David Barker

Shadows 10 – The Dead
by Paul Kane

Shadows 11 – The Forest of Dead Children
by Andrew Hook

Shadows 12 – At Home in the Shadows
by Gary McMahon

blackshuckbooks.co.uk/shadows